Charlotte Sebag-Montefiore

RIDDLES FROM THE AIR
Who am I?

Bumblebee Books
London

A CIP catalogue record for this title is
available from the British Library.

ISBN: 978-1-80439-325-3

This is a work of fiction.
Names, characters, places and incidents originate from the writer's
imagination. Any resemblance to actual persons, living or dead, is
purely coincidental.

Bumblebee Books is an imprint of
Olympia Publishers.

First Published in 2023

Bumblebee Books
Tallis House
2 Tallis Street
London
EC4Y 0AB

Printed in Great Britain

Dedicated to my dear husband

1

In Australia, we are black.
In Britain, we are white.
We swim and fly about by day
and sleep like you at night!

It's safer sleeping while afloat,
my head tucked in my wing.
On land there're many predators.
Safety's the main thing!

We are a large and heavy bird,
we can hurt you – keep away.
A wingspan nearly eight feet wide,
we're beautiful by day!

We're able to remember
if you've been kind before.
We're herbivores, and like to eat
fresh bread, green veg, for sure!

An ugly duckling, muddy brown,
I was when I was small.
That was what you called me once
I'm white now, lovely, tall!

Now that you have listened,
just tell me, what's my name?
If you don't know don't worry,
I'll tell you all the same!

2

I'm actually a beetle,
though you call me a bird.
I chomp a lot of insects,
pest control's the word!

I lay my eggs near aphids,
so that when they hatch,
my babies eat those insects
– whatever they can catch!

I've spots, to tell my predators
that I'm not good to eat.
They should leave me well alone.
I've nasty stinky feet!

Most of us are red with spots
but some are blue or pink.
We're really rather pretty,
at least that's what I think!

When it's cold, the aphids die,
it's time to hibernate.
Winter's coming, we must fly,
it's time for us to mate.

Now that you have listened,
just tell me, what's my name?
If you don't know don't worry,
I'll tell you all the same!

3

You know me by my lovely breast,
it's red when I am grown.
Sometimes you use it in my name,
it's that by which I'm known!

I nest in many places,
I'm not fussy as to where.
I'm practical – a basket, boot
– I use whatever's there!

Unlike some birds, I sing all year,
each and every day.
It lets the others know I'm there
I chase them all away!

My home is mine, I do not let
the other birds intrude.
I don't want others near, you see.
It's worms that are my food.

In winter, life is hard for me,
those worms are hard to spot.
Why not feed me berries, seeds?
I like them such a lot!

Now that you have listened,
just tell me, what's my name?
If you don't know don't worry,
I'll tell you all the same!

4

To look at, I am lovely,
white spots, some black, and dashing.
A brilliant orange when I fly
– I'm simply gorgeous, flashing!

I'm not a painted gent,
a lady, oh that's me!
I flutter by across the land,
I migrate across the sea!

My young live in a tent of silk.
On plants, it looks like fluff.
If thistles, there is food as well;
there's plenty, there's enough!

My predators are snakes and frogs,
and when they are around,
I close my wings – outside they're brown,
so that I can't be found!

No-one knows why we migrate,
we don't stick to a season.
We do not do it every year
but for an unknown reason!

Now that you have listened,
just tell me, what's my name?
If you don't know don't worry,
I'll tell you all the same!

5

We are the tallest flying birds.
We can fly pretty high,
at 30,000 feet or more,
an airplane in the sky!

Some of us migrate when
they want a change of scene.
Others stay somewhere they like,
somewhere that they have been!

We sleep when standing on one leg,
our head tucked in our wing.
We've lovely crests upon our heads,
we eat up anything!

Our courtship dance is famous,
we're faithful to our pair.
We're social and we fly in flocks
as we whizz through the air!

In Asia, we're a symbol
of happiness and youth,
elsewhere a sign of love and life
– yes, that is the truth!

Now that you have listened,
just tell me, what's my name?
If you don't know don't worry,
I'll tell you all the same!

6

My eyes are big and bulgy,
and I can see all round.
My four wings like to rest outspread
on wetlands, on the ground.

My wings are brilliant colours,
metallic – you can't miss them.
We skim and gobble insects,
we eat but do not kiss them!

As insects go, I'm pretty big.
My body's really long.
Some of us migrate quite far,
I'm really pretty strong.

My wings may hum to warm me up,
I may bathe in the sun!
If I am cold, I cannot hunt:
for predators, that's fun!

Sometimes we eat things half our weight,
and sometimes we do not.
What's certain is that we must eat
good food, and quite a lot!

Now that you have listened,
just tell me, what's my name?
If you don't know don't worry,
I'll tell you all the same!

7

Our memory is very good,
we must see and learn the way
to migrate south when it's too cold,
– we fly by night and day!

Two or three long thousand miles,
we have so far to go.
We cuddle for protection, warmth
– it's sensible, you know!

We form ourselves into a V
which helps the birds behind.
The shape is quite efficient;
this is what we find!

Our babies – we relate to them
when they are in the shell.
When they hatch, they take a day,
then they can swim quite well!

My cousins are the swans and ducks.
We've feelings just like you.
We grieve at loss – a partner,
you people do that too!

Now that you have listened,
just tell me, what's my name?
If you don't know don't worry,
I'll tell you all the same!

8

We've been here since the dinosaurs
– that's very long ago.
Our food, oh we like nectar,
we pollinate, you know!

ZZZ we buzz - that's what we do.
You know when we're about.
We like a nice big target,
nothing's wiped us out!

Movement, heat, and CO_2,
that's how we find our prey.
It takes us time to get there,
we're slow flyers – that's our way!

We do not all give you a bite,
our girls do, not our boys.
Girls need blood to grow their eggs;
our boys just make a noise!

We can make you very ill,
a lot of you will die.
Malaria, fevers, zika,
that is the reason why!

Now that you have listened,
just tell me, what's my name?
If you don't know don't worry,
I'll tell you all the same!

9

The Romans thought we brought good luck,
perhaps a baby too.
The Dutch and Germans agreed with this,
I do not know your view.

My wings can stretch out eight feet wide,
for some of us, it's more.
My bill snaps shut if there is food.
I am a carnivore!

Right down below the water,
it's murky, I can't see.
That's why I choose to hunt by touch,
it's a better way for me!

I may eat fish and froggies,
snakes, small mammals too.
How they wriggle to escape
– they very rarely do!

We keep the same nest every year
after our long migration.
If it needs to be repaired,
we work with application!

Now that you have listened,
just tell me, what's my name?
If you don't know don't worry,
I'll tell you all the same!

10

You may think I do not belong
to *Riddles from the Air.*
But I can fly for several miles,
so I *do* think it's fair!

Mostly I am on the earth
in cowpats or some dung.
We turn it into sausages
where we lay and hatch our young!

You may think it smelly,
we think it's really great!
Of all the animals on earth,
we're the strongest for our weight.

I use the stars to find my way,
you can do this too.
This is rare for insects,
it just is what we do!

We help recycle waste
which is needed and so good.
We help the food chain feed us all,
just as a food chain should!

Now that you have listened,
just tell me, what's my name?
If you don't know don't worry,
I'll tell you all the same!

11

Why work if you don't have to?
Yes, that's right – you heard!
I put my egg into a nest
built by another bird!

Each year I do lay lots of eggs,
maybe up to twenty.
I think you will agree with me
that is really plenty!

My lovely chicks hatch early,
they're the biggest in their brood.
They tip the other nestlings out,
so they get all the food!

That's why I choose for nurseries,
smaller birds than me.
Sparrows, perhaps wagtails,
they raise my chicks for free!

Maybe once they raised me too.
My egg does look like theirs.
A funny thing – not one of us
really knows or cares!

Now that you have listened,
just tell me, what's my name?
If you don't know don't worry,
I'll tell you all the same!

12

My body's mostly grey, except
my yellow beak, so bright.
My wingtips, smart, are tipped with black,
my head and belly's white!

We're scavengers and useful,
for we keep the beaches clean.
We eat almost anything, you see,
that is what I mean!

We mostly live in dumps inland.
That won't do for our nest.
We have to find a place that is
with scrumptious food, the best!

I don't like herring very much,
though you might think I do.
Seals and falcons eat me up,
I'm not at risk from you!

We have a loud and laughing call,
a very special sound.
To keep our nests safe from the wind,
we lay them on the ground!

Now that you have listened,
just tell me, what's my name?
If you don't know don't worry,
I'll tell you all the same!

13

I can fly so very fast,
I must, to catch my prey.
More than a hundred miles an hour,
I whizz and hunt by day!

It's not for nothing that they say,
"He has eyes like a hawk."
We see eight times as well as you,
we screech more than we squawk!

People used to ask for us
if they were very wise,
as ransom for a hostage,
we were a valued prize.

Once trained, we brought them food, you see,
everyone needs that.
A brace of tasty ducks, perhaps,
a rabbit or a rat!

They would eat the rabbit, ducks
and we would get the rat.
Sometimes we eat a squirrel, mouse,
a reptile, little cat!

Now that you have listened,
just tell me, what's my name?
If you don't know don't worry,
I'll tell you all the same!

14

My forelegs are the proper length,
and fold as if in prayer.
They've barbs to catch and grip my prey,
I'm lucky when it's there!

We like to eat the tasty moths
and flies, one then another,
insects, juicy ants as well,
sometimes we eat each other!

We bite our prey upon its neck
and gobble up its head.
It then has no escape from us,
it is completely dead!

Our predators are bats,
they find me very yummy.
I can hear them with my ear
in the middle of my tummy!

We can change our colour,
we can be brown or green.
Birds, bats and frogs may eat us up
we'd rather blend, unseen!

Now that you have listened,
just tell me, what's my name?
If you don't know don't worry,
I'll tell you all the same!

15

They say I am the bird of peace,
also, the bird of love.
It doesn't seem like that to me
when I fly up above!

I flew out from old Noah's ark
when the floods began to fall,
to see if there was land for us,
any land at all!

We are not really carnivores,
we eat all sorts of seed.
We do drink lots of water
to digest them as we need!

We have big wings and muscles,
our flying's very strong.
We use landmarks for signposts
if our journey's very long!

We're rather like the pigeon,
we do not like to roam.
With training, we take messages
and then we fly straight home!

Now that you have listened,
just tell me, what's my name?
If you don't know don't worry,
I'll tell you all the same!

16

A bird that cannot fly, that's me.
I'm white, my neck is long.
A huge bird, with eggs sized to match,
my legs are very strong.

I can kill lions with one kick.
I'm out by day, not night!
My breastbone's flat and that is why
I cannot soar in flight.

I lay my eggs with others,
I learn to know my own.
We lay them all together,
so that they're not alone!

Our partners help us with our eggs,
we sit on them in turn.
They're tasty for the predators
– that is our concern!

Sometimes I put my head right down,
I lay it on the sand.
Lions cannot see me then
– I'm sure you understand!

Now that you have listened,
just tell me, what's my name?
If you don't know don't worry,
I'll tell you all the same!

17

We were here before the dinosaurs,
millions of years ago.
Two or three hundred, really,
as our fossil records show.

Half our body weight in plants,
we need to eat each day.
We can destroy whole fields of crops
that simply is our way!

We're related to the cricket,
a jumping herbivore.
However far your athletes jump,
we can jump so much more!

Our hindlegs are like catapults,
but we can also fly.
This helps us flee from predators
– that is the reason why!

My ears are in a funny place
you'll find them on my tummy.
Sometimes people eat us up,
they find us very yummy!

Now that you have listened,
just tell me, what's my name?
If you don't know don't worry,
I'll tell you all the same!

18

We soar on thermal currents
to have a good look round.
We see what's dead a mile away,
we swoop down to the ground.

My legs and feet aren't strong enough
to carry off my prey.
Sometimes we have to wait to eat
till others have their way.

They open up the carcass,
there may be a rotten smell,
the poisonous germs don't hurt us,
so we can eat quite well!

We help you as we clean things up,
we keep disease at bay.
It's good when it is very hot,
you think so, anyway!

We're social and we roost in flocks.
If threatened, we are sick:
we spill out food and lighten up,
so fly a bit more quick!

Now that you have listened,
just tell me, what's my name?
If you don't know don't worry,
I'll tell you all the same!

19

You'll see a gorgeous shade of blue
as our four wings flutter by,
a deeper blue up north and west,
we are a butterfly!

You take the places where we live,
there are fewer of us here.
We like the grass and clearings
not the forest, trees or mere!

Our males like to defend their patch.
You'll see them quite a lot.
Our girls may hide themselves away
in a nice and lovely spot!

Our caterpillars bring the ants,
attracted by their smell.
This keeps the predators away,
it works out very well!

We shiver to get warm sometimes,
we can't fly when we're cold.
We're vulnerable when we are still,
we die when three weeks old!

Now that you have listened,
just tell me, what's my name?
If you don't know don't worry,
I'll tell you all the same!

20

We build our nests somewhere that's safe
on swamps or muddy dirt.
We don't want to be food ourselves,
be wounded or get hurt!

You people are a horrid threat,
you eat our eggs and tongue.
As parents we are pretty good,
take turns to feed our young!

Our little chicks, so fluffy,
start life a grey and white.
The food we give them turns them pink
they make a wondrous sight!

We've long necks, backward bending knees,
we're tall but very light.
We have to be, because, you see,
we may soar high in flight!

Our beaks sieve out the food we need.
They are a sort of spout,
and while we eat our lunch of shrimps,
the water dribbles out!

Now that you have listened,
just tell me, what's my name?
If you don't know don't worry,
I'll tell you all the same!

21

We build our nests round, like a ball,
with a hole we can get through.
It is just big enough for us,
not predators, nor you!

It's warmer if you face the south
we build our nests that way.
We're black and white and hop along,
we're active in the day!

Our predators get muddled.
We build more than one nest.
They do not know which one we'll choose,
though always it's the best!

We're clever, we can learn to count.
We're cousins to the crow.
We can use a broom to sweep
our nest – oh, did you know?

In packs, we work together
in defence against the cats,
foxes, owls and predators
and nasty vicious rats!

Now that you have listened,
just tell me, what's my name?
If you don't know don't worry,
I'll tell you all the same!

22

You mostly do not like me,
I have a nasty sting.
And I can use it lots of times,
I sting like anything!

Some of us live underground
– they like it on their own.
We mostly live in colonies
with a Queen upon our throne!

We come in many colours,
we're known for our small waist.
Nectar, insects, spiders
– that's all food to our taste!

You love figs which we pollinate,
that's something that we do.
And pest control of insects,
oh yes, we do that too!

Some birds do like to eat us,
a starling, sparrow, wren.
They bang us till our stinger drops
it's safe to eat us then!

Now that you have listened,
just tell me, what's my name?
If you don't know don't worry,
I'll tell you all the same!

23

We're sociable and that is why
we like to imitate.
We mimic sounds that we can hear,
so we communicate!

We mostly eat just nuts and plants,
with insects for our meat.
You eat with knives and forks and hands,
and we eat with our feet!

I'm clever and I can do sums,
I add up and subtract.
I know what zero means as well,
this simply is a fact!

We're faithful to our partners,
and mostly mate for life.
Our beak is really very strong
and sharp, just like a knife!

I've feelings like you people.
Sometimes I'm happy, sometimes sad,
and if my world is not quite right
I'm stressed when things are bad!

Now that you have listened,
just tell me, what's my name?
If you don't know don't worry,
I'll tell you all the same!

24

For several thousand years at least,
you've cultivated me.
Because I help your flowers and fruit
– that is why, you see!

My sense of smell is very good,
my eyesight is sharp too.
This helps me find the nectar
that I need for me and you!

I have got two tummies.
The first – food passes through;
the second keeps the nectar clean,
to reach my home like new!

I can only sting you once.
I'm going to tell you why:
your body tears my stinger out,
wounded, I must die!

Our girls buzz after nectar.
When they find it, they will dance.
This helps the others find it
very quickly – not by chance!

Now that you have listened,
just tell me, what's my name?
If you don't know don't worry,
I'll tell you all the same!

25

It cannot dig, crack nuts or fight,
it isn't very strong.
But oh, my beak's ginormous
it really is *so* long!

I am born without it,
it's too big for my shell!
I need my beak for camouflage
to keep me safe as well.

It's also very useful,
keeps my temperature just right,
exactly as I like it,
both by day and coolest night!

It has a sharp, serrated edge,
rather like a knife.
That's useful as it tears my food
or may defend my life!

My tail can flip and touch my head.
I'm famous for this too,
and for my gorgeous orange beak
that so appeals to you!

Now that you have listened,
just tell me, what's my name?
If you don't know don't worry,
I'll tell you all the same!

26

When we work together
as we always do,
we're superhuman in our strength
– much more so than you!

We haven't any lungs or ears.
Without them, we do well.
We feel vibrations through our feet,
communicate through smell.

Our colonies are huge sometimes,
– one Queen at least for sure.
The other girls do all the work
for food, the young, and more!

Some of us form armies and
hunt termites just like you.
We may eat lizards, spiders, frogs
as some of you do too!

We can run very quickly
and some of us can fly
to find a new home or a mate
– that is the reason why!

Now that you have listened,
just tell me, what's my name?
If you don't know don't worry,
I'll tell you all the same!

27

We're black, and bigger than a crow.
We're cleverer, like you.
We work in pairs, and learn to share
– which crows will never do!

We mimic human voices
of a woman or a man.
To have some fun, we may tease wolves
– oh yes, indeed we can!

We can learn and solve a problem.
We soar higher than a crow.
Some people think we bring bad news
do you think that's so?

We learn to know a cheater:
if another is unfair,
we never work with them again
we demand an equal share!

We point at things, make gestures
with our wings or with our beak.
Primates, humans do this too,
– but we can't quite speak!

Now that you have listened,
just tell me, what's my name?
If you don't know don't worry,
I'll tell you all the same!

28

We are not in the navy.
We're pretty, flutter by,
white spots, red bands, a dash of black.
Our life is short – we die!

We lay our eggs in nettles.
They make a leafy nest,
our caterpillars will eat the leaves
that they think taste the best!

We live around the whole wide world
and we might perch on you.
Do not brush us, we'll get hurt,
just puff or blow – please do!

Nectar is all that we eat.
We suck it through our straw
– it's known as our proboscis,
we suck up more and more!

Our colours, red and darkest black
look like a toxic punch.
We hope this way not to become
a predator's nice lunch!

Now that you have listened,
just tell me, what's my name?
If you don't know don't worry,
I'll tell you all the same!

29

I live in Britain through the year,
the only bird that's blue.
Woodlands or a garden home
– a nesting box will do!

Do not make the hole too big,
big birds might drive me out.
There's competition anyway,
there's lots of us about!

I can lay up to thirteen eggs,
quite a lot will die.
Climbing cats, starvation
– that is the reason why!

Our young find caterpillar moths
really very yummy.
We fly quite far to find them
to satisfy their tummy!

I am not very long or fat.
I am bluer when I'm old.
In summer we eat insects,
seeds too, when it is cold!

Now that you have listened,
just tell me, what's my name?
If you don't know don't worry,
I'll tell you all the same!

30

We are a friendly yellow bird
and other colours too.
Our boys do have a lovely song:
we like it – so do you!

My forebears from Madeira,
and those islands with my name
in the north Atlantic
– that is whence they came!

Coal miners took us down below,
we were their cheerful treasure.
We sang unless gas stopped us short
– we were their safety measure!

I do not mind it on my own,
though I need room to fly.
Like you, I do need exercise
– that is the reason why!

I need a lot of water,
seeds, insects and greens!
I sing a lot when happy,
that is what it means!

Now that you have listened,
just tell me, what's my name?
If you don't know don't worry,
I'll tell you all the same!

31

I am a special mammal,
the only one that flies.
You find me very spooky,
with my fangs and beady eyes!

Most of us eat insects,
but some of us do not.
One of us with pointy ears
likes sucking blood a lot!

We make high sounds that travel
till they hit something, bounce back.
It helps us find our food and route,
once you have the knack.

We've skin between our fingers,
we use our wings as cloaks.
We nest in holes and crevices,
in beech, and ash, and oaks!

We sleep and rest while upside down.
No-one quite knows why.
Some people think it is because
we must fall down to fly!

Now that you have listened,
just tell me, what's my name?
If you don't know don't worry,
I'll tell you all the same!

32

In Britain, for three months a year
we're here and in the air.
Except for when we mate and breed,
we even sleep up there!

Then we travel to the South,
flying swift and fast,
down to Southern Africa,
we do get there at last!

We've tiny feet, our legs are short,
the same mate every year.
Our boys and girls look just the same,
A *him* looks like a *her!*

In older buildings, there we nest
under eaves together.
We shelter in our colonies
from windy and wet weather!

But oh, if this lasts for too long,
our chicks may starve and die.
We cannot hunt on stormy days,
– that is the reason why!

Now that you have listened,
just tell me, what's my name?
If you don't know don't worry,
I'll tell you all the same!

33

We're bats and vegetarian,
our wingspan's five foot wide.
Without our pollination,
the eucalyptus would have died.

I am not a fox as such.
I certainly can fly.
If you read for clues below,
you'll find out who am I!

We used to live in groups
two hundred thousand strong.
Our colonies and camps, they used
to stretch some four miles long!

Extinction is a risk for us
on islands, and perhaps,
without us ecosystems
will fail and may collapse!

We like to find our food and fruit
by smelling in the air.
Because our eyesight's good as well
we find out what is there!

Now that you have listened,
just tell me, what's my name?
If you don't know don't worry,
I'll tell you all the same!

34

I'm wonderfully suited
to the life I have to lead.
My flattish face, uneven ears,
give me what I need!

I can see from so far off,
a distance, a long way,
I can hear just brilliantly
– this helps me catch my prey!

I've tufty feathers on my head
that look like twigs or leaves.
Camouflage! That's what it is,
it's brilliant, and deceives.

My prey can't see me till too late!
I do need lots of meat!
Near on a thousand mice a year,
that's what I like to eat!

Fish, and little birds I hunt
– in water and the skies.
I hoot and screech and turn my head
I cannot turn my eyes!

Now that you have listened,
just tell me, what's my name?
If you don't know don't worry,
I'll tell you all the same!

35

We love our homes, like you.
If you take them, we will die.
We don't move to another,
– that is the reason why!

Have you ever seen
on warm and summer nights
a show that seems in harmony
with lovely flashing lights?

That's us! we love the warmth,
grass, water and the night!
However else could we be seen?
We are a lovely sight!

Our lights are different colours,
yellow, orange, green!
Their message is "Don't eat us!"
that is what we mean!

As well as scaring predators,
our lights attract a mate.
They've got a pattern of their own
not too soon, not too late!

Now that you have listened,
just tell me, what's my name?
If you don't know don't worry,
I'll tell you all the same!

36

We are the largest birds of prey.
We have terrific sight,
much, much better than your own.
We do not hunt at night.

I have got transparent lids,
a see-through for my eyes.
When I fly extremely fast,
it protects them in the skies!

The wicked talons on my feet
can kill and carry prey.
My powerful beak's for eating,
I don't eat every day!

I might eat rabbits, squirrels, mice,
sometimes a little deer.
My shadow on its own's enough
to inspire flight and fear!

I mate for life. My nest is big,
it may be six foot wide.
The oldest, biggest chick may kill
the others by his side!

Now that you have listened,
just tell me, what's my name?
If you don't know don't worry,
I'll tell you all the same!

ANSWERS

1. Swan
2. Ladybird
3. Robin
4. Painted Lady
5. Crane
6. Dragonfly
7. Canada Goose
8. Mosquito
9. Stork
10. Dung Beetle
11. Cuckoo
12. Herring Gull
13. Hawk
14. Praying Mantis
15. Dove
16. Ostrich
17. Grasshopper
18. Vulture
19. Common Blue Butterfly
20. Flamingo
21. Magpie
22. Wasp
23. Parrot
24. Bee
25. Toucan
26. Ant
27. Raven
28. Red Admiral
29. Blue Tit
30. Canary
31. Vampire Bat
32. Swift
33. Flying Fox
34. Owl
35. Firefly
36. Eagle

About the Author

Charlotte Sebag-Montefiore worked for many years as an NHS clinical psychologist. This, and her family life, has helped her produce books which children love. She finds dinosaurs and animals very interesting... Charlotte combines her interest in animals with her love of rhyme and riddles in her earlier books *Who Am I? More Animal Riddles* and *Riddles from The Sea*. Her book *Herbie and The T. Rex* is about a dinosaur world where different dinosaur characters deal with the issues confronting them in their own way. Charlotte has returned to riddles and rhyme with this book, as she cannot resist them!